Jataka Tales

Ellen C. Babbitt

Title – Jataka Tales
Author – Ellen C. Babbitt
Publisher – EduGorilla Community Pvt. Ltd.

First Print

Publisher Address-
Sector-12/651, Indira Nagar, Lucknow,
Uttar Pradesh-226016
Tel: 91-6393 216806
Email: hello@edugorilla.com
www.facebook.com/edugorilladotcom
www.twitter.com/edugorilla
www.edugorilla.com/

ISBN: 9789355564481

Processed & printed in India

Preface

Jatakas means 'Birth,' it is a collection of extremely popular tales of the former lives of Buddha, these are preserved in all branches of Buddhism. Peter Skilling has quoted these as 'one of the oldest classes of Buddhist literature.' The Jatakas illustrate the many lives, acts and spiritual practices which are required on the long path to Buddhahood. These tales depict the future Buddha as a king, an outcast, an animal, and a deva, — but, in all forms, he exhibits some virtues that are thereby inculcated in the Jataka Tales.

Each Jataka tale starts by noting the occasion that prompted its telling and ends with the Buddha identifying the lives of the people in the introductory story with those of people from the past. Many Jatakas originate from the ancient Indian storytelling or narrative traditions that were both rich and varied.

Other than their appearance in the form of stories, many of these Jataka Tales have also been adopted for animated movies.

THE MONKEY AND THE CROCODILE

PART ONE

A monkey lived in a great tree on a riverbank.

In the river, there were many Crocodiles.

A Crocodile watched the Monkeys for a long time, and one day she said to her son: "My son, get one of those Monkeys for me. I want the heart of a Monkey to eat."

"How am I to catch a Monkey?" asked the little Crocodile. "I do not travel on land, and the Monkey does not go into the water."

"Put your wits to work, and you'll find a way," said the mother.

And the little Crocodile thought and thought.

At last, he said to himself: "I know what I'll do. I'll get that Monkey that lives in a big tree on the river bank. He wishes to go across the river to the island where the fruit is so ripe."

So the Crocodile swam to the tree where the Monkey lived. But he was a stupid Crocodile.

"Oh, Monkey," he called, "come with me over to the island where the fruit is so ripe."

"How can I go with you?" asked the Monkey. "I do not swim."

"No—but I do. I will take you over on my back," said the Crocodile.

The Monkey was greedy and wanted the ripe fruit, so he jumped down on the Crocodile's back.

"Off we go!" said the Crocodile.

"This is a fine ride you are giving me!" said the Monkey.

"Do you think so? Well, how do you like this?" asked the Crocodile, diving.

"Oh, don't!" cried the Monkey, as he went under the water. He was afraid to let go, and he did not know what to do under the water.

When the Crocodile came up, the Monkey sputtered and choked. "Why did you take me underwater, Crocodile?" he asked.

"I am going to kill you by keeping you underwater," answered the Crocodile. "My mother wants Monkey-heart to eat, and I'm going to take yours to her."

"Why did you take me underwater, Crocodile?" he asked.

"I wish you had told me you wanted my heart," said the Monkey, "then I might have brought it with me."

"How queer!" said the stupid Crocodile. "Do you mean to say that you left your heart back there in the tree?"

"That is what I mean," said the Monkey. "If you want my heart, we must go back to the tree and get it. But we are so near the island where the ripe fruit is, please take me there first."

"No, Monkey," said the Crocodile, "I'll take you straight back to your tree. Never mind the ripe fruit. Get your heart and bring it to me at once. Then we'll see about going to the island."

"Very well," said the Monkey.

But no sooner had he jumped onto the bank of the river than—whisk! up he ran into the tree.

From the topmost branches he called down to the Crocodile in the water below:

"My heart is way up here! If you want it, come for it, come for it!"

PART TWO

The monkey soon moved away from that tree.

He wanted to get away from the Crocodile so that he might live in peace.

But the Crocodile found him, far down the river, living in another tree.

In the middle of the river was an island covered with fruit trees.

Halfway between the bank of the river and the island, a large rock rose out of the water. The Monkey could jump to the rock, and then to the island. The Crocodile watched the Monkey crossing from the bank of the river to the rock, and then to the island.

He thought to himself, "The Monkey will stay on the island all day, and I'll catch him on his way home at night."

The Monkey had a fine feast, while the Crocodile swam about, watching him all day.

Toward night the Crocodile crawled out of the water and lay on the rock, perfectly still.

When it grew dark among the trees, the Monkey started for home. He ran down to the river bank, and there he stopped.

"What is the matter with the rock?" the Monkey thought to himself. "I never saw it so high before. The Crocodile is lying on it!"

But he went to the edge of the water and called: "Hello, Rock!"

No answer.

Then he called again: "Hello, Rock!"

Three times the Monkey called, and then he said: "Why is it, Friend Rock, that you do not answer me tonight?"

"Oh," said the stupid Crocodile to himself, "the rock answers the Monkey at night. I'll have to answer for the rock this time."

So he answered: "Yes, Monkey! What is it?"

The Monkey laughed, and said: "Oh, it's you, Crocodile, is it?"

"Yes," said the Crocodile. "I am waiting here for you. I am going to eat you."

"You have caught me in a trap this time," said the Monkey. "There is no other way for me to go home. Open your mouth wide so I can jump right into it."

The Monkey jumped.

Now the Monkey well knew that when Crocodiles open their mouths wide, they shut their eyes.

While the Crocodile lay on the rock with his mouth wide open and his eyes shut, the Monkey jumped.

But not into his mouth! Oh, no! He landed on the top of the Crocodile's head, and then sprang quickly to the bank. Up he whisked into his tree.

When the Crocodile saw the trick the Monkey had played on him, he said: "Monkey, you have great cunning. You know no fear. I'll let you alone after this."

"Thank you, Crocodile, but I shall be on the watch for you just the same," said the Monkey.

HOW THE TURTLE SAVED HIS OWN LIFE

A king once had a lake made in the courtyard for the young princes to play in. They swam about in it and sailed their boats and rafts on it. One day the king told them he had asked the men to put some fish into the lake.

Off the boys ran to see the fishes. Now, along with the fishes, there was a Turtle. The boys were delighted with the fishes, but they had never seen a Turtle, and they were afraid of it, thinking it was a demon. They ran back to their father, crying, "There is a demon on the bank of the lake."

The king ordered his men to catch the demon and bring it to the palace. When the Turtle was brought in, the boys cried and ran away.

The king was very fond of his sons, so he ordered the men who had brought the Turtle to kill it.

"How shall we kill it?" they asked.

"Pound it to powder," said someone. "Bake it in hot coals," said another.

"Throw the thing into the lake."

So one plan after another was spoken of. Then an old man who had always been afraid of the water said: "Throw the thing into the lake where it flows out over the rocks into the river. Then it will surely be killed."

When the Turtle heard what the old man said, he thrust out his head and asked: "Friend, what have I done that you should do such a dreadful thing as that to me? The other plans were bad enough, but to throw me into the lake! Don't speak of such a cruel thing!"

When the king heard what the Turtle said, he told his men to take the Turtle at once and throw it into the lake.

The Turtle laughed to himself as he slid away down the river to his old home. "Good!" he said, "those people do not know how safe I am in the water!"

THE MERCHANT OF SERI

There was once a merchant of Seri who sold brass and tinware. He went from town to town, in company with another man, who also sold brass and tinware. This second man was greedy, getting all he could for nothing, and giving as little as he could for what he bought.

When they went into a town, they divided the streets between them. Each man went up and down the streets he had chosen, calling, "Tinware for sale. Brass for sale." People came out to their doorsteps, and bought, or traded, with them.

In one house there lived a poor old woman and her granddaughter. The family had once been rich, but now the only thing they had left of all their riches was a golden bowl. The grandmother did not know it was a golden bowl, but she had kept this because her husband used to eat out of it in the old days. It stood on a shelf among the other pots and pans and was not often used.

He threw the bowl on the ground.

The greedy merchant passed this house, calling, "Buy my water-jars! Buy my pans!" The granddaughter said: "Oh, Grandmother, do buy something for me!"

"My dear," said the old woman, "we are too poor to buy anything. I have not anything to trade, even."

"Grandmother, see what the merchant will give for the old bowl. We do not use that, and perhaps he will take it and give us something we want for it."

The old woman called the merchant and showed him the bowl, saying, "Will you take this, sir, and give the little girl here something for it?"

The greedy man took the bowl and scratched its side with a needle. Thus he found that it was a golden bowl. He hoped he could get it for nothing, so he said: "What is this worth? Not even a halfpenny." He threw the bowl on the ground and went away.

By and by the other merchant passed the house. For it was agreed that either merchant might go through any street which the other had left. He called: "Buy my water-jars! Buy my tinware! Buy my brass!"

The little girl heard him and begged her grandmother to see what he would give for the bowl.

"My child," said the grandmother, "the merchant who was just here threw the bowl on the ground and went away. I have nothing else to offer in trade."

"But, Grandmother," said the girl, "that was a cross man. This one looks pleasant. Ask him. Perhaps he'll give some little tin dish."

"Call him, then, and show it to him," said the old woman.

As soon as the merchant took the bowl in his hands, he knew it was of gold. He said: "All that I have here is not worth so much as this bowl. It is a golden bowl. I am not rich enough to buy it."

"But, sir, a merchant who passed here a few moments ago, threw it on the ground, saying it was not worth a halfpenny, and he went away," said the grandmother. "It was worth nothing to him. If you value it, take it, giving the little girl some dish she likes for it."

But the merchant would not have it so. He gave the woman all the money he had and all his wares. "Give me but eight pennies," he said.

So he took the pennies and left. Going quickly to the river, he paid the boatman the eight pennies to take him across the river.

Soon the greedy merchant went back to the house where he had seen the golden bowl, and said: "Bring that bowl to me, and I will give you something for it."

"No," said the grandmother. "You said the bowl was worthless, but another merchant has paid a great price for it, and taken it away."

"It is a golden bowl."

Then the greedy merchant was angry, crying out, "Through this other man I have lost a small fortune. That bowl was of gold."

He ran down to the riverside, and, seeing the other merchant in the boat out in the river, he called: "Hallo, Boatman! Stop your boat!"

But the man in the boat said: "Don't stop!" So he reached the city on the other side of the river and lived well for a time on the money the bowl brought him.

THE TURTLE WHO COULDN'T STOP TALKING

A turtle lived in a pond at the foot of a hill. Two young wild Geese, looking for food, saw the Turtle, and talked with him. The next day the Geese came again to visit the Turtle and they became very well acquainted. Soon they were great friends.

"Friend Turtle," the Geese said one day, "we have a beautiful home far away. We are going to fly back to it tomorrow. It will be a long but pleasant journey. Will you go with us?"

"How could I? I have no wings," said the Turtle.

"Oh, we will take you, if only you can keep your mouth shut, and say not a word to anybody," they said.

"I can do that," said the Turtle. "Do take me with you. I will do exactly as you wish."

"How could I go with you?" said the Turtle.

So the next day the Geese brought a stick and they held the ends of it. "Now take the middle of this in your mouth, and don't say a word until we reach home," they said.

The Geese sprang into the air.

The Geese then sprang into the air, with the Turtle between them, holding fast to the stick.

The village children saw the two Geese flying along with the Turtle and cried out: "Oh, see the Turtle up in the air! Look at the Geese carrying a Turtle by a stick! Did you ever see anything more ridiculous in your life!"

The Turtle looked down and began to say, "Well, and if my friends carry me, what business is that of yours?" when he let go, and fell dead at the feet of the children.

As the two Geese flew on, they heard the people say, when they came to see the poor Turtle, "That fellow could not keep his mouth shut. He had to talk, and so lost his life."

"Oh, see the Turtle up in the air."

THE OX WHO WON THE FORFEIT

Long ago a man owned a very strong Ox. The owner was so proud of his Ox, that he boasted to every man he met about how strong his Ox was.

One day the owner went into a village, and said to the men there: "I will pay a forfeit of a thousand pieces of silver if my strong Ox cannot draw a line of one hundred wagons."

The men laughed, and said: "Very well; bring your Ox, and we will tie a hundred wagons in a line and see your Ox draw them along."

So the man brought his Ox into the village. A crowd gathered to see the sight. A hundred carts were in line, and the strong Ox was yoked to the first wagon.

Then the owner whipped his Ox, and said: "Get up, you wretch! Get along, you rascal!"

But the Ox had never been talked to in that way, and he stood still. Neither the blows nor the hard names could make him move.

"Get along, you rascal."

At last, the poor man paid his forfeit and went sadly home. There he threw himself on his bed and cried: "Why did that strong Ox act so? Many a time he has moved heavier loads easily. Why did he shame me before all those people?"

At last, he got up and went about his work. When he went to feed the Ox that night, the Ox turned to him and said: "Why did you whip me today? You never whipped me before. Why did you call me 'wretch' and 'rascal'? You never called me hard names before."

Then the man said: "I will never treat you badly again. I am sorry I whipped you and called you names. I will never do so anymore. Forgive me."

"Very well," said the Ox. "Tomorrow I will go into the village and draw the one hundred carts for you. You have always been a kind master until today. Tomorrow you shall gain what you lost."

The next morning the owner fed the Ox well and hung a garland of flowers about his neck. When they went into the village the men laughed at the man again.

They said: "Did you come back to lose more money?"

"Today I will pay a forfeit of two thousand pieces of silver if my Ox is not strong enough to pull the one hundred carts," said the owner.

So again the carts were placed in a line, and the Ox was yoked to the first. A crowd came to watch again. The owner said: "Good Ox, show how strong you are! You fine, fine creature!" And he patted his neck and stroked his sides.

A garland of flowers about his neck.

At once the Ox pulled with all his strength. The carts moved on until the last cart stood where the first had been.

Then the crowd shouted, and they paid back the forfeit the man had lost, saying: "Your Ox is the strongest Ox we ever saw."

And the Ox and the man went home, happy.

THE SANDY ROAD

Once upon a time a merchant, with his goods packed in many carts, came to a desert. He was on his way to the country on the other side of the desert.

The sun shone on the fine sand, making it as hot as the top of a stove. No man could walk on it in the sunlight. But at night, after the sun went down, the sand cooled, and then men could travel upon it.

So the merchant waited until after dark, and then set out. Besides the goods that he was going to sell, he took jars of water and of rice, and firewood, so that the rice could be cooked.

All night long he and his men rode on and on. One man was the pilot. He rode first, for he knew the stars, and by them, he guided the drivers.

At daybreak, they stopped and camped. They unyoked the oxen and fed them. They built fires and cooked the rice. Then they spread a great awning over all the carts and the oxen, and the men lay down under it to rest until sunset.

They built fires and cooked the rice.

In the early evening, they again built fires and cooked rice. After supper, they folded the awning and put it away. They yoked the oxen, and, as soon as the sand was cool, they started again on their journey across the desert.

Night after night they traveled in this way, resting during the heat of the day. At last one morning, the pilot said: "In one more night we shall get out of the sand." The men were glad to hear this, for they were tired.

After supper that night the merchant said: "You may as well throw away nearly all the water and the firewood. By tomorrow we shall be in the city. Yoke the oxen and start on."

Then the pilot took his place at the head of the line. But, instead of sitting up and guiding the drivers, he lay down in the wagon on the cushions. Soon he was fast asleep, because he had not slept for many nights, and the light had been so strong in the daytime that he had not slept well then.

All night long the oxen went on. Near daybreak, the pilot awoke and looked at the last stars fading in the light. "Halt!" he called to the drivers. "We are in the same place where we were yesterday. The oxen must have turned about while I slept."

They unyoked the oxen, but there was no water for them to drink. They had thrown away the water that was left the night before. So the men spread the awning over the carts, and the oxen lay down, tired and thirsty. The men, too, lay down saying, "The wood and water are gone—we are lost."

But the merchant said to himself, "This is no time for me to sleep. I must find water. The oxen cannot go on if they do not have water to drink. The men must have water. They cannot cook the rice unless they have water. If I give up, we shall all be lost!"

"There must be water somewhere below."

On and on he walked, keeping close watch of the ground. At last, he saw a tuft of grass. "There must be water somewhere below, or that grass would not be there," he said.

He ran back, shouting to the men, "Bring the spade and the hammer!"

They jumped up and ran with him to the spot where the grass grew. They began to dig, and by and by they struck a rock and could dig no further. Then the merchant jumped down into the hole they had dug and put his ear to the rock. "I hear water running under this rock," he called to them. "We must not give up!" Then the merchant came up out of the hole and said to a serving lad: "My boy if you give up we are lost! You go down and try!"

The boy stood up straight and raised the hammer high above his head and hit the rock as hard as ever he could. He would not give in. They must be saved. Down came the hammer. This time the rock broke. And the boy had hardly time to get out of the well before it was full of cool water. The men drank as if they never could get enough, and then they watered the oxen and bathed.

Then they split up their extra yokes and axles, built a fire, and cooked their rice. Feeling better, they rested through the day. They set up a flag on the well for travelers to see.

At sundown, they started on again, and the next morning reached the city, where they sold the goods, and then returned home.

THE QUARREL OF THE QUAILS

Once upon a time, many quails lived together in a forest. The wisest of them all was their leader.

A man lived near the forest and earned his living by catching quails and selling them. Day after day he listened to the note of the leader calling the quails. By and by this man, the fowler, was able to call the quails together. Hearing the note the quails thought it was their leader who called.

When they were crowded together, the fowler threw his net over them, and off he went into the town, where he soon sold all the quails that he had caught.

The wise leader saw the plan of the fowler for catching the quails. He called the birds to him and said, "This fowler is carrying away so many of us, we must put a stop to it. I have thought of a plan; it is this: The next time the fowler throws a net over you, each of you must put your head through one of the little holes in the net. Then all of you together must fly away to the nearest thorn bush. You can leave the net on the thorn bush and be free yourselves."

The quails said that was a very good plan and they would try it the next time the fowler threw the net over them.

The very next day the fowler came and called them together. Then he threw the net over them. The quails lifted the net and flew away with it to the nearest thorn bush where they left it. They flew back to their leader to tell him how well his plan had worked.

The fowler was busy until evening getting his net off the thorns and he went home empty-handed. The next day the same thing happened, and the next. His wife was angry because he did not bring home any money, but the fowler said, "The fact is those quails are working together now. The moment my net is over them, off they fly with it, leaving it on a thorn bush. As soon as the quails begin to quarrel I shall be able to catch them."

Not long after this, one of the quails in alighting on their feeding ground, trod by accident on another's head. "Who trod on my head?" angrily cried the second. "I did, but I didn't mean to. Don't be angry," said the first quail, but the second quail was angry and said mean things.

The quails lifted the net and flew away with it.

Soon all the quails had taken sides in this quarrel. When the fowler came that day he flung his net over them, and this time instead of flying off with it, one side said, "Now, you lift the net," and the other side said, "Lift it yourself."

"You try to make us lift it all," said the quails on one side. "No, we don't!" said the others, "you begin and we will help," but neither side began.

So the quails quarreled, and while they were quarreling the fowler caught them all in his net. He took them to town and sold them for a good price.

The fowler caught them all in his net.

THE MEASURE OF RICE

At one time a dishonest king had a man called the Valuer in his court. The Valuer set the price which ought to be paid for horses and elephants and the other animals. He also set the price on jewelry and gold, and things of that kind.

This man was honest and just and set the proper price to be paid to the owners of the goods.

The king was not pleased with this Valuer, because he was honest. "If I had another sort of a man as Valuer, I might gain more riches," he thought.

One day the king saw a stupid, miserly peasant come into the palace yard. The king sent for the fellow and asked him if he would like to be the Valuer. The peasant said he would like the position. So the king had him made Valuer. He sent the honest Valuer away from the palace.

Then the peasant began to set the prices on horses and elephants, upon gold and jewels. He did not know their value, so he would say anything he chose. As the king had made him a Valuer, the people had to sell their goods for the price he set.

So they went before the king.

By and by a horse dealer brought five hundred horses to the court of this king. The Valuer came and said they were worth a mere measure of rice. So the king ordered the horse dealer to be given the measure of rice, and the horses to be put in the palace stables.

The horse dealer went then to see the honest man who had been the Valuer and told him what had happened.

"What shall I do?" asked the horse dealer.

"I think you can give a present to the Valuer which will make him do and say what you want him to do and say," said the man. "Go to him and give him a fine present, then say to him: 'You said the horses are worth a measure of rice, but now tell what a measure of rice is worth! Can you value that standing in your place by the king?' If he says he can go with him to the king, and I will be there, too."

The horse dealer thought this was a good idea. So he took a fine present to the Valuer and said what the other man had told him to say.

The Valuer took the present and said: "Yes, I can go before the king with you and tell what a measure of rice is worth. I can value that now."

"Well, let us go at once," said the horse dealer. So they went before the king and his ministers in the palace.

The horse dealer bowed down before the king and said: "O King, I have learned that a measure of rice is the value of my five hundred horses. But will the king be pleased to ask the Valuer what is the value of the measure of rice?"

He ran away from the laughing crowd.

The king, not knowing what had happened, asked: "How now, Valuer, what are five hundred horses worth?"

"A measure of rice, O King!" said he.

"Very good, then! If five hundred horses are worth a measure of rice, what is the measure of rice worth?"

"The measure of rice is worth your whole city," replied the foolish fellow.

The ministers clapped their hands, laughing, and saying, "What a foolish Valuer! How can such a man hold that office? We used to think this great city was beyond price, but this man says it is worth only a measure of rice."

Then the king was ashamed and drove out the foolish fellow.

"I tried to please the king by setting a low price on the horses, and now see what has happened to me!" said the Valuer, as he ran away from the laughing crowd.

THE FOOLISH, TIMID RABBIT

Once upon a time, a Rabbit was asleep under a palm tree.

All at once he woke up, and thought: "What if the world should break up! What then would become of me?"

At that moment, some Monkeys dropped a cocoanut. It fell down on the ground just back of the Rabbit.

Hearing the noise, the Rabbit said to himself: "The earth is all breaking up!"

And he jumped up and ran just as fast as he could, without even looking back to see what made the noise.

He jumped up and ran.

Another Rabbit saw him running, and called after him, "What are you running so fast for?"

"Don't ask me!" he cried.

But the other Rabbit ran after him, begging to know what was the matter.

The lion.

Then the first Rabbit said: "Don't you know? The earth is all breaking up!"

And on the ran, and the second Rabbit ran with him.

The next Rabbit they met ran with them when he heard that the earth was all breaking up.

One Rabbit after another joined them until there were hundreds of Rabbits running as fast as they could go.

They passed a Deer, calling out to him that the earth was all breaking up. The Deer then ran with them.

Saw the animals running.

The Deer called to a Fox to come along because the earth was all breaking up.

On and on they ran, and an Elephant joined them.

At last, the Lion saw the animals running, and heard their cry that the earth was all breaking up.

He thought there must be some mistake, so he ran to the foot of a hill in front of them and roared three times.

This stopped them, for they knew the voice of the King of Beasts, and they feared him.

"Why are you running so fast?" asked the Lion.

"Oh, King Lion," they answered him, "the earth is all breaking up!"

"Who saw it breaking up?" asked the Lion.

"I didn't," said the Elephant. "Ask the Fox—he told me about it."

"I didn't," said the Fox.

"The Rabbits told me about it," said the Deer.

One after another the Rabbits said: "I did not see it, but another Rabbit told me about it."

At last, the Lion came to the Rabbit who had first said the earth was all breaking up.

"Is it true that the earth is all breaking up?" the Lion asked.

"Yes, O Lion, it is," said the Rabbit. "I was asleep under a palm tree. I woke up and thought, 'What would become of me if the earth should all break up?' At that very moment, I heard the sound of the earth breaking up, and I ran away."

"Then," said the Lion, "you and I will go back to the place where the earth began to break up, and see what is the matter."

So the Lion put the little Rabbit on his back, and away they went like the wind. The other animals waited for them at the foot of the hill.

The Rabbit told the Lion when they were near the place where he slept, and the Lion saw just where the Rabbit had been sleeping.

He saw, too, the cocoanut that had fallen to the ground nearby. Then the Lion said to the Rabbit, "It must have been the sound of the cocoanut falling to the ground that you heard. You foolish Rabbit!"

And the Lion ran back to the other animals and told them all about it.

If it had not been for the wise King of Beasts, they might be running still.

Away they went like the wind.

THE WISE AND THE FOOLISH MERCHANT

Once upon a time in a certain country, a thrifty merchant visited a great city and bought a great supply of goods. He loaded wagons with the goods, which he was going to sell as he traveled through the country.

A stupid young merchant was buying goods in the same city. He, too, was going to sell what he bought as he traveled through the country.

They were both ready to start at the same time.

The thrifty merchant thought, "We cannot travel together, for the men will find it hard to get wood and water, and there will not be enough grass for so many oxen. Either he or I ought to go first."

So he went to the young man and told him this, saying, "Will you go before or come on after me?"

The other one thought, "It will be better for me to go first. I shall then travel on a road that is not cut up. The oxen will eat grass that has not been touched. The water will be clean. Also, I shall sell my goods at what price I like." So he said, "Friend, I will go on first."

This answer pleased the thrifty merchant. He said to himself, "Those who go before will make the rough places smooth. The old rank grass will have been eaten by the oxen that have gone before, while my oxen will eat the freshly grown tender shoots. Those who go before will dig wells from which we shall drink. Then, too, I will not have to bother about setting prices, but I can sell my goods at the prices set by the other man." So he said aloud, "Very well, friend, you may go on first."

At once the foolish merchant started on his journey. Soon he had left the city and was in the country. By and by he came to a desert which he had to cross. So he filled great water jars with water, loaded them into a large wagon, and started across the desert.

Now on the sands of this desert there lived a wicked demon. This demon saw the foolish young merchant coming and thought to himself, "If I can make him empty those water-jars, soon I shall be able to overcome him and have him in my power."

So the demon went further along the road and changed himself into the likeness of a noble gentleman. He called up a beautiful carriage, drawn by milk-white oxen. Then he called ten other demons, dressed them like men, and armed them with bows and arrows, swords and shields. Seated in his carriage, followed by the ten demons, he rode back to meet the merchant. He put mud on the carriage wheels, and hung water-lilies and wet grasses upon the oxen and the carriage. Then he made the clothes the demons wore and their hair all wet. Drops of water trickled down over their faces just as if they had all come through a stream.

As the demons neared the foolish merchant they turned their carriage to one side of the way, saying pleasantly, "Where are you going?"

The merchant replied, "We have come from the great city back there and are going across the desert to the villages beyond. You come dripping with mud and carrying water-lilies and grasses. Does it rain on the road you have come by? Did you come through a stream?"

He put mud on the carriage wheels, and hung water-lilies and wet grasses upon the oxen and the carriage.

The demon answered, "The dark streak across the sky is a forest. In it, there are ponds full of water-lilies. The rains come often. What have you in all those carts?"

"Goods to be sold," replied the merchant.

"But in that last big heavy wagon what do you carry?" the demon asked.

"Jars full of water for the journey," answered the merchant.

The demon said, "You have done well to bring water as far as this, but there is no need for it beyond. Empty out all that water and go on easily." Then he added, "But we have delayed too long. Drive on!" And he drove on until he was out of sight of the merchant. Then he returned to his home with his followers to wait for the night to come.

The foolish merchant did as the demon bade him and emptied every jar, saving not even a cupful. On and on they traveled and the streak on the sky faded with the sunset. There was no forest, the dark line being only clouds. No water was to be found. The men had no water to drink and no food to eat, for they had no water in which to cook their rice, so they went thirsty and supperless to bed. The oxen, too, were hungry and thirsty and dropped down to sleep here and there.

Late at night, the demons fell upon them and easily carried off every man. They drove the oxen on ahead of them, but the loaded carts they did not care to take away.

A month and a half after this the wise merchant followed over the same road. He, too, was met in the desert by the demon just as the other had been. But the wise man knew the man was a demon because he cast no shadow. When the demon told him of the ponds in the forest ahead and advised him to throw away the water jars the wise merchant replied, "We don't throw away the water we have until we get to a place where we see there is more."

Then the demon drove on. But the men who were with the merchant said, "Sir! those men told us that yonder was the beginning of a great forest, and from there onwards it was always raining. Their clothes and hair were dripping with water. Let us throw away the water-jars and go on faster with lighter carts!"

Stopping all the carts the wise merchant asked the men, "Have you ever heard anyone say that there was a lake or pond in this desert? You have lived near here always."

"We never heard of a pond or lake," they said.

"Does any man feel a wind laden with dampness blowing against him?" he asked.

"No, sir," they answered.

"Can you see a rain cloud, any of you?" said he.

"No, sir, not one," they said.

"Those fellows were not men, they were demons!" said the wise merchant. "They must have come out to make us throw away the water. Then when we were faint and weak they might have put an end to us. Go on at once and don't throw away a single half-pint of water."

He himself with the headmen stood on guard.

So they drove on and before nightfall, they came upon the loaded wagons belonging to the foolish merchant.

Then the thrifty merchant had his wagons drawn up in a circle. In the middle of the circle, he had the oxen lie down, and also some of the men. He himself with the headmen stood on guard, swords in hand, and waited for the demons. But the demons did not bother them. Early the next day the thrifty merchant took the best of the wagons left by the foolish merchant and went on safely to the city across the desert.

There he sold all the goods at a profit and returned with his company to his own city.

THE ELEPHANT GIRLY-FACE

Once upon a time, a king had an Elephant named Girly-face. The Elephant was called Girly-face because he was so gentle and good and looked so kind. "Girly-face never hurts anybody," the keeper of the Elephants often said.

Now one night some robbers came into the courtyard and sat on the ground just outside the stall where Girly-face slept. The talk of the robbers awoke Girly-face.

"This is the way to break into a house," they said. "Once inside the house kill anyone who wakens. A robber must not be afraid to kill. A robber must be cruel and have no pity. He must never be good, even for a moment."

Girly-face said to himself, "Those men are teaching me how I should act. I will be cruel. I will show no pity. I will not be good—not even for a moment."

The talk of the robbers awoke Girly-face.

He picked him up in his trunk and threw the poor keeper to the ground.

So the next morning when the keeper came to feed Girly-face he picked him up in his trunk and threw the poor keeper to the ground, killing him.

Another keeper ran to see what the trouble was, and Girly-face killed him, too.

For days and days, Girly-face was so ugly that no one dared go near. The food was left for him, but no man would go near him.

By and by the king heard of this and sent one of his wise men to find out what ailed Girly-face.

The wise man had known Girly-face a long time. He looked the Elephant over carefully and could find nothing that seemed to be the matter.

He thought at last, "Girly-face must have heard some bad men talking. Have there been any bad men talking about here?" asked the wise man.

"Yes," one of the keepers said, "a band of robbers was caught here a few weeks ago. They had met in the yard to talk over their plans. They were talking together near the stall where Girly-face sleeps."

He looked the Elephant over carefully.

So the wise man went back to the king. Said he, "I think Girly-face has been listening to the bad talk. If you will send some good men to talk where Girly-face can hear them I think he will be a good Elephant once more."

So that night the king sent a company of the best men to be found to sit and talk near the stall where Girly-face lived. They said to one another, "It is wrong to hurt anyone. It is wrong to kill. Everyone should be gentle and good."

"Now those men are teaching me," thought Girly-face. "I must be gentle and good. I must hurt no one. I must not kill anyone." And from that time on Girly-face was tame and as good as ever an Elephant could be.

THE BANYAN DEER

There was once a Deer the color of gold. His eyes were like round jewels, his horns were white as silver, his mouth was red like a flower, and his hoofs were bright and hard. He had a large body and a fine tail.

He lived in a forest and was king of a herd of five hundred Banyan Deer. Nearby lived another herd of Deer, called the Monkey Deer. They, too, had a king.

The king of that country was fond of hunting the Deer and eating deer meat. He did not like to go alone so he called the people of his town to go with him, day after day.

The townspeople did not like this for while they were gone no one did their work. So they decided to make a park and drive the Deer into it. Then the king could go into the park and hunt and they could go on with their daily work.

They made a park, planted grass in it and provided water for the Deer, built a fence all around it, and drove the Deer into it.

Then they shut the gate and went to the king to tell him that in the park nearby he could find all the Deer he wanted.

The king went at once to look at the Deer. First, he saw there the two Deer kings and granted them their lives. Then he looked at their great herds.

Some days the king would go hunting the Deer, sometimes his cook would go. As soon as any of the Deer saw them they would shake with fear and run. But when they had been hit once or twice they would drop down dead.

The King of the Banyan Deer sent for the King of the Monkey Deer and said, "Friend, many of the Deer are being killed. Many are wounded besides those who are killed. After this suppose one from my herd goes up to be killed one day, and the next day let one from your herd go up. Fewer Deer will be lost this way."

The King of the Banyan Deer sent for the King of the Monkey Deer.

The Monkey Deer agreed. Each day the Deer whose turn it was would go and lie down, placing its head on the block. The cook would come and carry off the one he found lying there.

One day the lot fell to a mother Deer who had a young baby. She went to her king and said, "O King of the Monkey Deer, let the turn pass me by until my baby is old enough to get along without me. Then I will go and put my head on the block."

But the king did not help her. He told her that if the lot had fallen to her she must die.

Then she went to the King of the Banyan Deer and asked him to save her.

"Go back to your herd. I will go in your place," said he.

The next day the cook found the King of the Banyan Deer lying with his head on the block. The cook went to the king, who came himself to find out about this.

"King of the Banyan Deer! did I not grant you your life? Why are you lying here?"

"O great King!" said the King of the Banyan Deer, "a mother came with her young baby and told me that the lot had fallen to her. I could not ask anyone else to take her place, so I came myself."

Rise up. I grant your life and hers.

"King of the Banyan Deer! I had never seen such kindness and mercy. Rise up. I grant your life and hers. Nor will I hunt any more the Deer in either park or forest."

THE PRINCES AND THE WATER-SPRITE

Once upon a time, a king had three sons. The first was called Prince of the Stars. The next was called the Moon Prince and the third was called the Sun Prince. The king was so very happy when the third son was born that he promised to give the queen any boon she might ask.

The queen kept the promise in mind, waiting until the third son was grown before asking the king to give her the boon.

On the twenty-first birthday of the Sun Prince, she said to the king, "Great King, when our youngest child was born you said you would give me a boon. Now I ask you to give the kingdom to Sun Prince."

But the king refused, saying that the kingdom must go to the oldest son, for it belonged by right to him. Next, it would belong by right to the second son, and not until they were both dead could the kingdom go to the third son.

The queen went away, but the king saw that she was not pleased with his answer. He feared that she would do harm to the older princes to get them out of the way of the Sun Prince.

So he called his elder sons and told them that they must go and live in the forest until his death. "Then come back and reign in the city that is yours by right," he said. And with tears, he kissed them on the foreheads and sent them away.

As they were going down out of the palace, after saying goodbye to their father, the Sun Prince called to them, "Where are you going?"

And when he heard where they were going and why, he said, "I will go with you, my brothers."

So off they started. They went on and on and by and by they reached the forest. There they sat down to rest in the shade of a pond. Then the eldest brother said to Sun Prince, "Go down to the pond and bathe and drink. Then bring us a drink while we rest here."

Now the King of the Fairies had given this pond to a water-sprite. The Fairy King had said to the water-sprite, "You are to have in your power all who go down into the water except those who give the right answer to one question. Those who give the right answer will not be in your power. The question is, 'What are the Good Fairies like?'"

The Sun Prince went into the pond.

When the Sun Prince went into the pond the water-sprite saw him and asked him the question, "What are the Good Fairies like?"

"They are like the Sun and the Moon," said the Sun Prince.

"You don't know what the Good Fairies are like," cried the water-sprite, and he carried the poor boy down into his cave.

By and by the eldest brother said, "Moon Prince, go down and see why our brother stays so long in the pond!"

As soon as the Moon Prince reached the water's edge the water-sprite called to him and said, "Tell me what the Good Fairies are like!"

"Like the sky above us," replied the Moon Prince.

"You don't know, either," said the water-sprite, and dragged the Moon Prince down into the cave where the Sun Prince sat.

"Something must have happened to those two brothers of mine," thought the eldest. So he went to the pond and saw the marks of the footsteps where his brothers had gone down into the water. Then he knew that a water-sprite must live in that pond. He girded on his sword and stood with his bow in his hand.

The water-sprite soon came along in the form of a woodsman.

"You seem tired, Friend," he said to the prince. "Why don't you bathe in the lake and then lie on the bank and rest?"

The water sprite is in the form of a woodsman.

But the prince knew that it was a water sprite and he said, "You have carried off my brothers!"

"Yes," said the water-sprite.

"Why did you carry them off?"

"Because they did not answer my question," said the water-sprite, "and I have power over all who go down into the water except those who do give the right answer."

"I will answer your question," said the eldest brother. And he did. "The Good Fairies are like

The pure in heart who fear to sin,
The good, kindly in word and deed."

"O Wise Prince, I will bring back to you one of your brothers. Which shall I bring?" said the water-sprite.

"Bring me the younger one," said the prince. "It was on his account that our father sent us away. I could never go away with Moon Prince and leave poor Sun Prince here."

"O Wise Prince, you know what the good should do and you are kind. I will bring back both your brothers," said the water-sprite.

After that, the three princes lived together in the forest until the king died. Then they went back to the palace. The eldest brother was made king and he had his brothers rule with him. He also built a home for the water-sprite on the palace grounds.

THE KING'S WHITE ELEPHANT

Once upon a time, a number of carpenters lived on a riverbank near a large forest. Every day the carpenters went in boats to the forest to cut down the trees and make them into lumber.

One day while they were at work an Elephant came limping on three feet toward them. He held up one foot and the carpenters saw that it was swollen and sore. Then the Elephant lay down and the men saw that there was a great splinter in the sore foot. They pulled it out and washed the sore carefully so that in a short time it would be well again.

Thankful for the cure, the Elephant thought: "These carpenters have done so much for me, I must be useful to them."

So after that, the Elephant used to pull up trees for the carpenters. Sometimes when the trees were chopped down he would roll the logs down to the river. Other times he brought their tools for them. And the carpenters used to feed him well morning, noon, and night.

He held up one foot and the carpenters saw that it was swollen and sore.

Now, this Elephant had a son who was white all over—a beautiful, strong young one. Said the old Elephant to himself, "I will take my son to the place in the forest where I go to work each day so that he may learn to help the carpenters, for I am no longer young and strong."

The Elephant used to pull up trees for the carpenters.

So the old Elephant told his son how the carpenters had taken good care of him when he was badly hurt and took him to them. The white Elephant did as his father told him to do and helped the carpenters and they fed him well.

When the work was done at night the young Elephant went to play in the river. The carpenters' children played with him, in the water and on the bank. He liked to pick them up in his trunk and set them on the high branches of the trees and then let them climb down on his back.

With a last look at his playmates, the beautiful white Elephant went on with the king.

One day the king came down the river and saw this beautiful white Elephant working for the carpenters. The king at once wanted the Elephant for his own and paid the carpenters a great price for him. Then with a last look at his playmates, the children, the beautiful white Elephant went on with the king.

The king was proud of his new Elephant and took the best care of him as long as he lived.

THE OX WHO ENVIED THE PIG

Once upon a time, there was an Ox named Big Red. He had a younger brother named Little Red. These two brothers did all the carting on a large farm.

Now the farmer had an only daughter and she was soon to be married. Her mother gave orders that the Pig should be fattened for the wedding feast.

Little Red noticed that the Pig was fed on choice food. He said to his brother, "How is it, Big Red, that you and I are given only straw and grass to eat, while we do all the hard work on the farm? That lazy Pig does nothing but eating the choice food the farmer gives him."

Said his brother, "My dear Little Red, envy him not. That little Pig is eating the food of death! He is being fattened for the wedding feast. Eat your straw and grass and be content and live long."

Little Red noticed that the Pig was fed on choice food.

The fattened Pig was killed and cooked for the wedding feast.

Not long afterward the fattened Pig was killed and cooked for the wedding feast.

Then Big Red said, "Did you see, Little Red, what became of the Pig after all his fine feeding?"

"Yes," said the little brother, "we can go on eating plain food for years, but the poor little Pig ate the food of death and now he is dead. His feed was good while it lasted, but it did not last long."

GRANNY'S BLACKIE

Once upon a time, a rich man gave a baby Elephant to a woman.

She took the best of care of this great baby and soon became very fond of him.

The children in the village called her Granny, and they called the Elephant "Granny's Blackie."

The Elephant carried the children on his back all over the village. They shared their goodies with him and he played with them.

"Please, Blackie, give us a swing," they said to him almost every day.

"Come on! Who is first?" Blackie answered and picked them up with his trunk, swung them high in the air, and then put them down again, carefully.

But Blackie never did any work.

He ate and slept, played with the children, and visited with Granny.

One day Blackie wanted Granny to go off to the woods with him.

Blackie swung them high in the air.

"I can't go, Blackie, dear. I have too much work to do."

Then Blackie looked at her and saw that she was growing old and feeble.

"I am young and strong," he thought. "I'll see if I cannot find some work to do. If I could bring some money home to her, she would not have to work so hard."

So next morning, bright and early, he started down to the river bank.

There he found a man who was in great trouble. There was a long line of wagons so heavily loaded that the oxen could not draw them through the shallow water.

When the man saw Blackie standing on the bank he asked, "Who owns this Elephant? I want to hire him to help my Oxen pull these wagons across the river."

A child standing nearby said, "That is Granny's Blackie."

"Very well," said the man, "I'll pay two pieces of silver for each wagon this Elephant draws across the river."

Blackie was glad to hear this promise. He went into the river and drew one wagon after another across to the other side.

Then he went up to the man for the money.

The man counted out one piece of silver for each wagon.

When Blackie saw that the man had counted out but one piece of silver for each wagon, instead of two, he would not touch the money at all. He stood in the road and would not let the wagons pass him.

The man tried to get Blackie out of the way, but not one step would he move.

Then the man went back and counted out another piece of silver for each of the wagons and put the silver in a bag tied around Blackie's neck.

Then Blackie started for home, proud to think that he had a present for Granny.

The children had missed Blackie and had asked Granny where he was, but she said she did not know where he had gone.

They all looked for him but it was nearly night before they heard him coming.

"Where have you been, Blackie? And what is that around your neck?" the children cried, running to meet their playmate.

He would not touch the money at all.

Blackie told her that he had earned some money for her.

But Blackie would not stop talking with his playmates. He ran straight home to Granny.

"Oh, Blackie!" she said, "Where have you been? What is in that bag?" And she took the bag off his neck.

Blackie told her that he had earned some money for her.

"Oh, Blackie, Blackie," said Granny, "how hard you must have worked to earn these pieces of silver! What a good Blackie you are!"

And after that Blackie did all the hard work and Granny rested, and they were both very happy.

THE CRAB AND THE CRANE

In the Long Ago, there was a summer when very little rain fell.

All the Animals suffered for want of water, but the Fishes suffered most of all.

In one pond full of fish, the water was very low indeed.

A Crane sat on the bank watching the Fishes.

"What are you doing?" asked a little Fish.

"I am thinking about you Fishes there in the pond. It is so nearly dry," answered the Crane.

"Yes," the Crane went on, "I was wishing I might do something for you. I know of a pond in the deep woods where there is plenty of water."

"I declare," said the little Fish, "you are the first Crane that ever offered to help a Fish."

"That may be," said the Crane, "but the water is so low in your pond. I could easily carry you one by one on my back to that other pond where there is plenty of water and food and cool shade."

"I don't believe there is any such pond," said the little Fish. "What you wish to do is to eat us, one by one."

"If you don't believe me," said the Crane, "send with me one of the Fishes whom you can believe. I'll show him the pond and bring him back to tell you all about it."

A big Fish heard the Crane and said, "I will go with you to see the pond—I may as well be eaten by the Crane as to die here."

So the Crane put the big Fish on his back and started for the deep woods.

Soon the Crane showed the big Fish the pool of water. "See how cool and shady it is here," he said, "and how much larger the pond is, and how full it is!"

"Yes!" said the big Fish, "take me back to the little pond and I'll tell the other Fishes all about it." So back they went.

The Fishes all wanted to go when they heard the big Fish talk about the fine pond which he had seen.

So the Crane put the big Fish on his back and started for the deep woods.

Then the Crane picked up another Fish and carried it away. Not to the pool, but into the woods where the other Fishes could not see them.

Then the Crane put the Fish down and ate it. The Crane went back for another Fish. He carried it to the same place in the woods and ate it, too.

This he did until he had eaten all the fish in the pond.

The next day the Crane went to the pond to see if he had left a Fish. There was no one left, but there was a Crab on the sand.

"Little Crab," said the Crane, "would you let me take you to the fine pond in the deep woods where I took the Fishes?"

"But how could you carry me?" asked the Crab.

"Oh, easily," answered the Crane. "I'll take you on my back as I did the Fishes."

"No, I thank you," said the Crab, "I can't go that way. I am afraid you might drop me. If I could take hold of your neck with my claws, I would go. You know we Crabs have a tight grip."

The Crane knew about the tight grip of the Crabs, and he did not like to have the Crab hold on with his claws. But he was hungry, so he said:

"Very well, hold tight."

And off went the Crane with the Crab.

And off went the Crane with the Crab.

When they reached the place where the Crane had eaten the Fishes, the Crane said:

"I think you can walk the rest of the way. Let go of my neck."

"I see no pond," said the Crab. "All I can see is a pile of Fishbones. Is that all that is left of the Fishes?"

"Yes," said the Crane, "and if you will let go of my neck, your shell will be all that will be left of you."

And the Crane put his head down near the ground so that the Crab could get off easily.

But the Crab pinched the Crane's neck so that his head fell off.

"Not my shell, but your bones are left to dry with the bones of the Fishes," said the Crab.

WHY THE OWL IS NOT KING OF THE BIRDS

Why is it that Crows torment the Owls as they sleep in the daytime? For the same reason that the Owls try to kill the Crows while they sleep at night.

Listen to a tale of long ago and then you will see why.

Once upon a time, the people who lived together when the world was young took a certain man for their king. The four-footed animals also took one of their number for their king. The fish in the ocean chose a king to rule over them. Then the birds gathered together on a great flat rock, crying:

"Among men, there is a king, and among the beasts, and the fish have one, too; but we birds have none. We ought to have a king. Let us choose one now."

And so the birds talked the matter over and at last, they all said, "Let us have the Owl for our king."

"See how sour he looks right now."

No, not all, for one old Crow rose up and said, "For my part, I don't want the Owl to be our king. Look at him now while you are all crying that you want him for your king. See how sour he looks right now. If that's the cross look he wears when he is happy, how will he look when he is angry? I, for one, want no such sour-looking king!"

Then the Crow flew up into the air crying, "I don't like it! I don't like it!" The Owl rose and followed him. From that time on the Crows and the Owls have been enemies. The birds chose a Turtle Dove to be their king and then flew to their homes.